What's Bugging nurse Penny?

A Story about Lice

Catherine Stier

illustrated by
Suzanne Beaky

Albert Whitman & Company
Chicago, Illinois

To the dedicated school nurses who safeguard the health and well-being of our children. You are appreciated!—**C.S.**

To Moofus and Doofus—**S.B.**

Library of Congress Cataloging-in-Publication Data

Stier, Catherine.
What's bugging Nurse Penny? / by Catherine Stier ;
illustrated by Suzanne Beaky.
p. cm.
Summary: When Nurse Penny loses her smile, three of her
young patients provide encouragement, which leads to an
impromptu school assembly at which Nurse Penny educates
students about head lice, with which she, herself, is afflicted.
ISBN 978-0-8075-8803-1 (hardcover)
[1. School nursing—Fiction. 2. Lice—Fiction. 3. Schools—
Fiction.] I. Beaky, Suzanne, 1971- illustrator. II. Title. III.
Title: What is bugging Nurse Penny?
PZ7.S8556295Wh 2013 [E]—dc23 2013001663

Text copyright © 2013 by Catherine Stier
Illustrations copyright © 2013 by Suzanne Beaky
Published in 2013 by Albert Whitman & Company.

Printed in China.
10 9 8 7 6 5 4 3 2 1 NP 18 17 16 15 14 13

The design is by Carol Gildar.

For more information about Albert Whitman & Company,
visit our web site at www.albertwhitman.com.

Nurse Penny, our school nurse, can deal with *anything*.

Blisters. Bloody noses. Bee stings. Tummy aches, headaches, and earaches.

"Eureka!" Nurse Penny whoops when she figures out what's wrong. "We'll banish this trouble in no time!" Then she does a winner's fist pump.

But one afternoon, Nurse Penny looked glum. As she spoke on the telephone, she even...scowled.

"That's not at all like Nurse Penny," I whispered to Tessa and Van.

Tessa had lost a tooth and needed one of Nurse Penny's take-home-your-tooth treasure chests.

Van held ice on his bumped knee.

As for me, it was almost time for my medicine.

"Max, Tessa, what do you think is bugging Nurse Penny?" Van whispered back.

Both Tessa and I shrugged.

"Children," said Nurse Penny, "the substitute nurse will be caring for you today. I'm going home." Then she headed for the door.

I stood up. "Nurse Penny, we hope things get better soon!" I said as cheerily as I could.

Nurse Penny stopped.

"Now, my bright learners, what makes you think something is wrong?" she asked.

"Something chased away your smile," I said.

"Chased it far away," agreed Van.

"Whatever it is, Nurse Penny, we know you will banish this trouble in no time!" Tessa said. Then she did a winner's fist pump.

One side of Nurse Penny's mouth quivered up. Then the other.

"Eureka!" Nurse Penny whooped. "My oh-so-smart students are right! I will banish this trouble in no time. And I'm proud as can be of you three. Thanks to your kindness, I just had an inspiration!" She scooted into the principal's office.

"An inspiration?" Van asked.
Tessa and I shrugged.

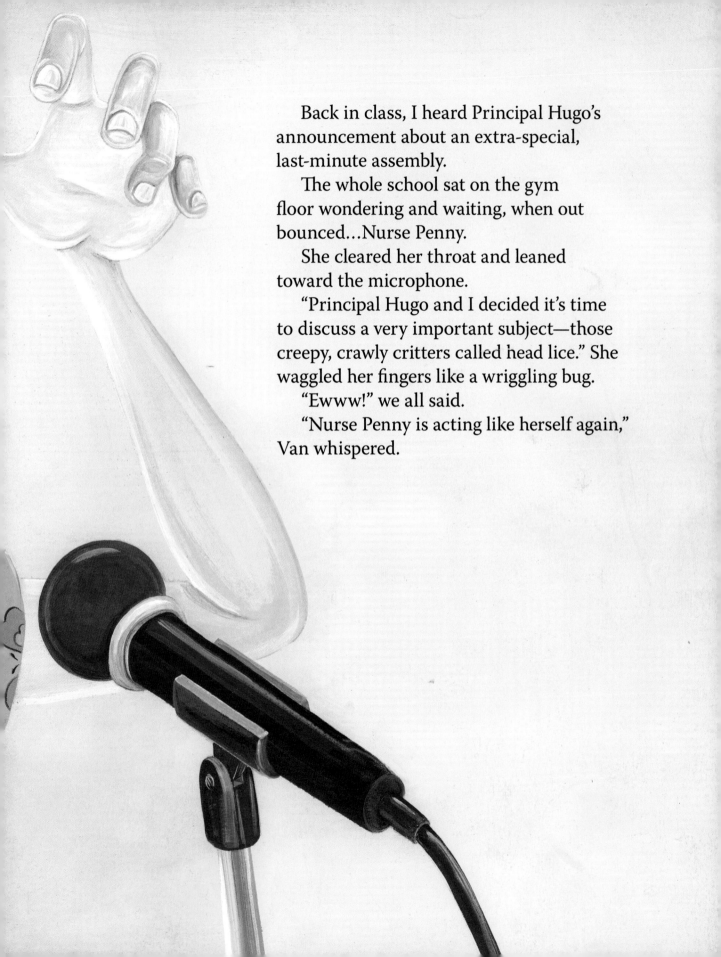

Back in class, I heard Principal Hugo's announcement about an extra-special, last-minute assembly.

The whole school sat on the gym floor wondering and waiting, when out bounced...Nurse Penny.

She cleared her throat and leaned toward the microphone.

"Principal Hugo and I decided it's time to discuss a very important subject—those creepy, crawly critters called head lice." She waggled her fingers like a wriggling bug.

"Ewww!" we all said.

"Nurse Penny is acting like herself again," Van whispered.

"Nobody wants to get lice," said Nurse Penny. "They show up uninvited and make a home in your hair. They make your head itch. They can make you grumpy.

"So let's find out what lice look like, what they do, and how to avoid the sneaky little nuisances."

Nurse Penny unrolled a poster. "A louse— that's a single bug—has six legs and no wings. Lice are a brownish, grayish color. They are tiny—only about one-eighth of an inch long."

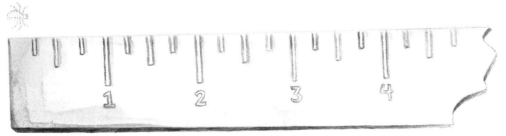

"Head lice have been around a long time," Nurse Penny continued. "Scientists have even found signs of lice on mummies!

"As small as they are," Nurse Penny said, "when lice crawl around your hair, they can make you itch like crazy!"

A girl raised her hand. "Imagine a werewolf with lice!" she said and giggled.

"As a matter of fact," said Nurse Penny, "lice aren't interested in animals like cats or dogs—or wolves. But they love hanging around people. Know why?" Nurse Penny paused. "Because they feed on…human blood."

Tessa raised her hand. "Like Dracula?" she asked.

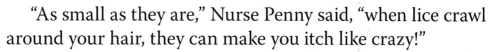

"More like a mosquito than Dracula," Nurse Penny said. "Except lice don't fly away. To get rid of lice, there are special treatments your doctor can recommend. The treatment goes on your hair and helps get those bugs out.

"But lice leave behind eggs, or nits, that don't wash away. That's because lice stick their eggs to human hair with amazing insect superglue! To get rid of the eggs, you have to comb them out."

"So how do you stop a lice invasion?" I asked.

"Magnificent question, Max!" Nurse Penny said. "Some of you might think keeping your hair super squeaky clean will keep them away." Nurse Penny shook her head. "These pesky little bugs don't care about all the grooming you do."

"Here are some tips:

"Since lice can crawl from one person's hair to another's, don't lean too close together over a book or at the computer.

"Don't share things like combs or brushes.

"Don't trade hats or hoodies or hair bows.

"But the very most important don't of all is—*don't feel bad!* When lice move in, it's a nuisance. It's uncomfortable. Definitely yucky. But they shouldn't chase away your smile."

"Chase away your smile?" I whispered to Tessa and Van. "Do you think…?"

"Having a case of lice is nothing to feel embarrassed about," said Nurse Penny. "It can happen to kids who play in the mud, and kids who stay neat as a pin.

"It can happen to grown-ups like parents and teachers.
And it can happen to…the school nurse!"
Everyone became really quiet.
"Yep, even to me," Nurse Penny said.

"How did I get them? Could be from a movie theater seat. Or a hat I tried on at the mall. Or most likely from someone in my own family. I don't know for sure.

"So right now, my office is being cleaned and vacuumed to send those bugs packing. And I'm heading home. I'll use a special lice treatment, and I'll follow the directions very carefully.

"And very soon, I'll be back at school doing my favorite job in the world—being your school nurse!"
Nurse Penny bowed.
Everybody clapped wildly.

Later, Tessa and Van and I met at the After School Art Club. I pulled out the crayons, markers, and glitter.

"Nurse Penny said she was proud of us, and that we gave her an inspiration," I said. "But I'm proud of her. And she gave me an inspiration—one I'll share with you two. Now, how do you spell *eureka*?"

NURSE

When Nurse Penny came to school on Monday morning, Tessa, Van, and I were waiting outside her office.

"Hello, my stupendous scholars," Nurse Penny said. "I've banished those bugs and I'm back!"

"We know why you told your story at Friday's assembly," I said. "So that if any more of us ever have to deal with lice, we won't feel bad. And we think that was brave!"

"Fearless," added Van.

"Noble, even," said Tessa.

And then I pushed open Nurse Penny's office door.

Nurse Penny saw our inspiration: pictures—lots of pictures, taped all over. We had drawn Nurse Penny as a brave astronaut, a fearless superhero, a noble queen. We made pictures of her shouting "Eureka!" and doing a winner's fist pump. And always, always smiling.

Nurse Penny's office gleamed as bright as her ladybug bag, as colorful as her butterfly smock, as sparkly as her honeybee earrings.

"Oh, my astounding artists," said Nurse Penny with a sniff and the biggest smile yet, "how beautiful!"

Some Facts about Lice

* A single lice bug is called a louse. An adult louse may grow to two or three millimeters long. That's about the size of a sesame seed.

* Lice may appear light gray or tan in color.

* Female lice can lay up to ten eggs a day. They attach each egg with a glue-like substance to a human hair shaft near the scalp.

* Lice eggs hatch in eight or nine days. Once the eggs hatch, the empty shells, or nits, are left behind and remain attached to the hair shaft.

* Lice feed every few hours. They inject a small amount of saliva and draw out a small amount of blood from a person's scalp.

* The most common symptom of a lice infestation is an itchy scalp.

* Lice do not spread disease.

* A lice infestation is not a sign of uncleanliness.

* Lice infestation is most common in children three to twelve years old. However, adults may be infested too.

* Lice infestation in the United State is less common in African Americans. According to the United States Centers for Disease Control and Prevention website "the head louse found most frequently in the United States may have claws that are better adapted for grasping the shape and width of some types of hair but not others."

These facts are based on information from an online clinical report from the American Academy of Pediatrics, with additional information from the website of the United States Centers for Disease Control and Prevention.

pediatrics.aappublications.org/content/126/2/392.full.pdf+html

www.cdc.gov/parasites/lice/head/biology.html